HOW DO YOU HUG A PORCUPINE?

¿CÓMO ABRAZAS A UN PUERCOESPÍN?

By / Por
Laurie Isop

Illustrated by / Ilustrado por
Gwen Millward

SCHOLASTIC INC.
New York Toronto London Auckland
Sydney Mexico City New Delhi Hong Kong

To my father, Ron Austin, who always gave the very best hugs
—L. I.

To Myfanwy, with love
—G. M.

Acknowledgments
Thank you to Paul, Austin, and Erik for tolerating my prickly
side, and to my dear family and friends—Debbie, Joyce, Cheryl,
Annette, Anh-Thu, Ping, Sandi, Maria, Suresh, Richard,
Mark, and Gregg—for believing in me.
—L. I.

No part of this publication may be reproduced, stored in a retrieval system, or transmitted in any
form or by any means, electronic, mechanical, photocopying, recording, or otherwise, without
written permission of the publisher. For information regarding permission, write to Simon &
Schuster Books for Young Readers, an imprint of Simon & Schuster Children's Publishing Division,
1230 Avenue of the Americas, New York, NY 10020.

ISBN 978-0-545-45410-0

Text copyright © 2011 by Laurie Isop. Illustrations copyright © 2011 by Gwen Millward.
Translation by Argentina Palacios Ziegler. All rights reserved. Published by Scholastic Inc.,
557 Broadway, New York, NY 10012, by arrangement with Simon & Schuster Books for Young
Readers, an imprint of Simon & Schuster Children's Publishing Division. Cheerios® is a
registered trademark of General Mills. SCHOLASTIC and associated logos are
trademarks and/or registered trademarks of Scholastic Inc.

12 11 10 9 8   16 17/0

Printed in the U.S.A.   40

First Scholastic printing, January 2012

Book design by Chloë Foglia
The text for this book is set in Barcelona.
The illustrations for this book were rendered in lead-based pencil,
watercolor paint, and acrylic ink on Daler-Rowney heavyweight paper.
Inspiration was provided by Gwen's pet rabbit and muse, Saskia (a.k.a. Sassy the bun).

Can you hug a horse?
Of course!

¿Aun caballo lo puedes abrazar?
¡Pues no faltaba más!

A cow?
With arms around her neck,
that's how.

¿A una vaca?
Con los brazos en el pescuezo,
así es eso.

A dog or cat is not so hard.

No es difícil ni un perro ni un gato.

Just hug them in your own backyard.

En tu patio les puedes dar un abrazo.

Hugging bunnies is just divine.

Abrazar a los conejitos es realmente divino.

But how do you hug a porcupine?

¿Pero cómo abrazas a un puercoespín?

Can you hug some billy goats?
Entice them with a bag of oats!

¿A los chivos los puedes abrazar?
¡Con avena los puedes interesar!

And surely you can hug a pig;
just spread your arms out
EXTRA big.

Y por seguro a un cerdo puedes abrazar,
sólo abres los brazos
A TODO dar.

With baby chicks
be sweet, be kind.

A los pollitos trata
con dulzura y ternura.

But how do you hug

¿Pero cómo abrazas

a porcupine?

a un puercoespín?

This prickly fellow won't be easy.
(My stomach's feeling kind of queasy!)

He wears a coat of thorny quills.
To hug this one will take some skills!

Este tipo espinoso mucha faena va a dar.
(¡Hasta me han dado ganas de vomitar!)

De púas espinosas es su coraza.
¡Para abrazar a éste necesitas habilidad!

A hedgehog is
a little prickly.

Un erizo es
algo espinoso.

An ostrich is
a little tickly.

Un avestruz es
algo cosquillo

A chimpanzee
will hug you back.

Un chimpancé
te corresponde el abrazo.

I've never tried
to hug a yak.

Abrazar a un yak
yo jamás lo he intentado.

A giraffe requires quite a climb.

Una jirafa requiere tremenda subida.

But how do you hug a porcupine?

¿Pero cómo abrazas a un puercoespín?

An elephant?
Please hug his trunk.

¿A un elefante?
Sólo la trompa le debes abrazar.

I wouldn't want to hug a skunk!

¡A un zorrillo no me gustaría abrazar!

A kangaroo?
Just hop this way!

¿A un canguro?
¡Sólo salta para acá!

Don't let the dolphins
slip away!

¡A los delfines no los
dejes escapar!

A panda probably
wouldn't mind.

Tal vez no le importe
a un panda.

But how do you hug a porcupine?

¿Pero cómo abrazas a un puercoespín?

You must go slowly; never hurry.

Debes andar despacio, nunca de prisa.

Porcupines aren't soft and furry.

El puercoespín no es suavecito ni peludito

His quills defend him from his foes,

De sus enemigos sus púas lo defienden,

but I'm his friend, he surely knows.

pero yo soy su amigo, sin duda él lo entiende.

At last! Hooray! It's finally time!

¡Por fin! ¡Hurra! ¡La hora ha llegado!

THIS is how you hug a porcupine:

ASÍ es como abrazas a un puercoespín:

CAREFULLY!

¡CON TODO CUIDADO!